W9-AWL-617

SOPHIE the SWEETHEART

☆

Finding the right name isn't easy!
See what else Sophie tries out....

1: SOPHIE the AWESOME

2: SOPHIE the HERO

3: SOPHIE the CHATTERBOX

4: SOPHIE the ZILLIONAIRE

5: SOPHIE the SNOOP

6: SOPHIE the DAREDEVIL

7: SOPHIE the SWEETHEART

SOPHIE the SWEETHEART

by Lara Bergen

illustrated by Laura Tallardy

SCHOLASTIC INC.

New York Toronto London Auckland
Sydney Mexico City New Delhi Hong Kong

For the REAL Sophie the Sweetheart,
Sophie Joyce Miller

No part of this publication may be reproduced, stored in a retrieval system, or transmitted in any form or by any means, electronic, mechanical, photocopying, recording, or otherwise, without written permission of the publisher. For information regarding permission, write to Scholastic Inc., Attention: Permissions Department, 557 Broadway, New York, NY 10012.

ISBN 978-0-545-33074-9

12 11 10 9 8 7 6 5 4 3 2 1   11 12 13 14 15 16/0

Printed in the U.S.A.   40
First printing, November 2011
Designed by Tim Hall

CHAPTER 1

Dear Ms. Moffly,
  I love you.
  Will you marry me?
  Sinseerly, Mr. Bloom

There. Sophie put down her pen. *That should work!* She grinned. Then she turned to her best friend, Kate Barry. Did she agree?

It was all part of their big plan, a plan they'd just made that afternoon in Sophie's room. A plan to get their third-grade teacher, Ms.

Moffly, to marry the fifth-grade teacher, Mr. Bloom.

At first, Kate had thought it was a little crazy. "Ms. Moffly?" she said. "And Mr. Bloom? Doesn't he wear *jeans*? Do you think Ms. Moffly's ever worn those?"

Then Sophie explained how much the two had in common: "They both teach at Ordinary Elementary School!"

And she pointed out how cool it would be if they got married: "That means a wedding! And of course that means we get to go!"

"Oh!" That made Kate's eyebrows bounce. Then she thought of something, too. "Hey! Know what else that means?"

"What?"

"It means a honeymoon!"

Sophie nodded. "You're right! Do you think we'd get to go on that?"

"Probably not." Kate shrugged. "But it might mean no school."

Oh. Well, that was almost as good. It fact, it

was pretty great. But not as great as the other thing Sophie hoped this plan would bring: an awesome, perfect name!

Sophie was tired — *exhausted*, even — of being Sophie the Most Average Girl in the Whole School. And she was determined to start being Sophie the... *anything*. Anything that made her stand out from the rest of the world.

And now she had the best idea! She had gotten it at the end of school that day. Ms. Moffly had been struggling with a box, and Sophie had run up to help.

"Sophie, you are such a sweetheart," Ms. Moffly had told her.

And that was it!

Sophie the Sweetheart! Who could ask for a better name than that? All she had to do was keep being sweet and helpful to Ms. Moffly. And everybody else. It shouldn't be too hard, Sophie figured. Not as hard as some other names had been. She was pretty good at being sweet — she just forgot now and then.

Of course, she had run the name by Kate first. "Ooh! I like it!" Kate said. "It makes me think of Cupid! All you need are some wings and a bow and arrow. Then you could make everyone fall in love!"

Sophie wasn't going to go *that* far. But it did give her a great idea. What could be sweeter than helping Ms. Moffly get a sweetheart of her own? Someone like Mr. Bloom ... to help her carry boxes at home, too!

"So do you think it's okay?" Sophie asked Kate, holding up the letter for them both to read.

Kate nodded. "Yeah, it sounds good. Unless you want to use a joke."

"Like what?" asked Sophie.

Kate raised her eyebrows and grinned. "Like, knock-knock."

"Who's there?"

"Howard."

"Howard who?"

"Howard you like to marry me?" Kate giggled and slapped Sophie's back.

Sophie smiled, but she rolled her eyes, too. "Good one. But I don't think so."

"Suit yourself." Kate grinned and read the note again. Then a thought seemed to grow inside her. She scratched a freckle on her neck.

"What?" Sophie asked.

"The handwriting," Kate said.

Huh? Sophie studied the page. "I tried to be so neat. And look, there's a heart above the 'i.'" She could have written in cursive, she guessed. But those *f*'s were so tricky.

"I think it might be *too* neat," Kate said. "Grown-up writing never looks as neat as that."

Oh . . . right. Sophie thought about her mom's handwriting. That was a mess.

"Okay." She reached for a clean sheet of paper. "Let me try again."

"Hang on. There's something else," Kate said.

Sophie froze her pen.

Kate went on. "I wonder if we should use first names. Like maybe say 'Dear Lila' instead."

"Good idea!" said Sophie, nodding hard. Why hadn't she thought of that?

"'Dear *Lila* . . .'" She started writing. Then she stopped. "Uh-oh. Do you know what Mr. Bloom's first name is?" she asked Kate.

Kate did not. Too bad.

But someone else does! Sophie remembered. That someone walked in right then.

"Hayley!"

Sophie's big sister just happened to be in Mr. Bloom's class. Sophie waved the pen as her sister brushed past her bed. "We have a very important question for you!" she said.

Hayley kept walking toward her dresser. "No, I will *not* play Monopoly with you," she declared. "You guys always gang up against me, and it takes way too long. Besides, I'm here because I have to change for ballet. So you have to go right now."

Sophie sighed. She wished that, just once,

Hayley would remember this was her room, too. But she wasn't going to let that bother her. At least, not much.

"Don't worry. That wasn't our question," Sophie told her. "We just want to know Mr. Bloom's first name."

Hayley opened her top drawer and pulled out a leotard. "Mike." Then she turned as Sophie started to scribble. "Why do you want to know?"

"Well..." Sophie shared a look with Kate. They both shrugged at the same time. *Why not tell Hayley?* Sophie thought. She would find out soon enough!

"Here! You can read for yourself." She proudly showed Hayley her new letter. "I'm going to give it to Ms. Moffly. And she'll think that it's from...*Mike*. And when they get married, they'll invite everybody. Your class, too, I bet! And they'll live happily ever after. It's pretty *sweet* of me, don't you think?"

She waited for Hayley to answer. She was excited — and nervous, too. She knew that this was a great idea. But Hayley didn't always see at first how great Sophie's ideas were.

Hayley's mouth twisted sideways. "This is interesting," she said.

Yes! Sophie took the letter back. Hayley liked her idea!

"I wonder if they'll ask their best students to be in the wedding," Hayley went on.

Be in the wedding? Ooh! "Like a flower girl?" Sophie asked. She had always wanted to be one of those!

Hayley nodded, then looked in the mirror and smiled. "You third graders might be flower girls. I'd be a junior bridesmaid, though."

"Oh, I hope it's not a long engagement!" said Sophie. She tried to do the math in her head. "Let's see. . . . If I give this note to Ms. Moffly first thing in the morning, how long will it take? A week?"

That was when Hayley's eyes got serious again. She turned back to Sophie and said very sternly, "You cannot give that note to her."

"It's my handwriting, isn't it?" Sophie sighed. "I know. It's too neat."

Hayley shook her head. "Mr. Bloom's handwriting is a lot messier, yes. But that's not it. I'm talking about what happens when Ms. Moffly says, 'Yes.' And Mr. Bloom says, 'Huh?' because he doesn't even know he asked."

Oh.

Sophie nodded. "I see," she said, thinking hard. "So do you think the note should be from Ms. Moffly instead?"

"No." Hayley shook her head again. "Don't you read or watch TV? People go on *dates* first, Sophie. They don't just get married."

"They don't?" Sophie frowned. She thought that was exactly what they did.

"No." Hayley rolled her eyes, and she grabbed some tights from her drawer. "You'll know that when you're ten."

Sophie turned to Kate. She could tell this was news to her, too. But if Ms. Moffly and Mr.

Bloom had to go out on a *date* first, then that was what they would do.

Sophie slapped the paper down on her lap desk. Then she took her pen and went back to work.

Dear ~~Ms. Moffly~~ Lila,
  I love you.
  Will you ~~marry me?~~ go on a date with me?
  Sinseerly, ~~Mr. Bloom~~ Mike
  P.S. Then will you marry me?

When she was done, Sophie showed it to Hayley. "Better?" she asked.

Hayley slowly shook her head.

"Don't worry," Sophie said quickly. "I'll type it up so it looks official."

"Here's another idea," Hayley said with a sigh. "Ask Mom to invite them both to dinner." Then she looked at the clock. "Now get out. I have to change or I'll be late!"

"Whatever you say!" Sophie hopped off her bed. For once, she didn't complain. She grabbed Kate's hand and dragged her out the door. "We have a whole new plan to make!"

"Wow," Kate said. "Your sister sure knows a lot about love."

"Yep!" Sophie grinned proudly. "It must be in our blood!"

CHAPTER 2

Sophie and Kate hurried downstairs.

"Mom! *Mom!*" Sophie cried.

"I'm in the kitchen!" her mom yelled back. "And remember, no yelling in the house!"

Sophie followed her mom's voice and found her at the kitchen table with Sophie's little brother, Max. That was no surprise. But what they were doing there was a *big* surprise.

"Mom!" Sophie gasped. "I didn't think you were going to let Max have Play-Doh again!"

"I know." Her mom sighed. "But he found it

in the cabinet today, so I thought we'd give it one more try."

Sophie looked down at the table. It was covered with blobs of bright dough. Then she looked at her two-year-old brother. He was covered with twice as much.

"Just as long as he doesn't eat it," Sophie's mom went on. "Right, Maxy? No mouth!" she warned.

Of course, as soon as she said that, Max scooped up a big blue hunk of dough. Then he slowly lifted it near his mouth and flashed a sneaky look.

"Oh, Maxy, you're too much!" Sophie's mom gave him a hug. Then she turned back, smiling, to Sophie and Kate. "So, what do you girls want?"

One thing Sophie wanted was for her mom to stop spoiling Max. If only Max could have stayed a baby. He had been so cute and sweet back then! He had just sat there and held Sophie's finger. Or played peekaboo. But now he ran and jumped and climbed on stuff and threw Cheerios and peas. He was turning into a regular maniac. He needed a trainer. And a leash.

But that wasn't why Sophie was standing there with Kate.

"Mom?" she said, very sweetly. "I have a . . . *request*. I think we should invite Ms. Moffly and Mr. Bloom over for dinner. Could we? Please?"

Sophie squeezed Kate's hand while she waited for the answer. And she thought about what sweet thing to say if her mom said, "No way."

But to her surprise, her mom nodded. "That's a nice idea, Sophie. Okay."

Yes! Sophie swung Kate's hand. It was a date!

"Let's see," her mom went on. "Maybe sometime after break. . . ."

"Wait!" Sophie stopped her. They couldn't wait that long! "How about tomorrow?"

Her mom's eyes grew wide and scared. "Tomorrow?! No, Sophie. Definitely not."

"Then how about Friday?" Sophie begged. She almost got down on her knees. But she knew better than to let her hair get too close to Max. She'd made that mistake before!

Her mom replied by laughing her you-crazy-kids laugh. But after a second, it turned into a regular smile. She rolled some Play-Doh between her hands and thought. "Ms. Moffly and Mr. Bloom...on *Friday*? Well, I guess we can see about that."

Hooray! Sophie hugged Kate. Then she started to hug her mom. But before she could, Max jumped down with two handfuls of Play-Doh and took off.

"Come back with that, mister!" Sophie's mom called. But by then, he was out of the room. She went running after him. "Don't let that dough get on the rug! And don't step on it! Oh, *no* . . ."

Sophie winced.

"That doesn't sound good," said Kate.

"It never is," Sophie agreed. She sighed, then

picked up some Play-Doh and slid into Max's seat.

Kate sat down, too. "I haven't played with this in forever. *Mmm!* Remember that smell? I think I'll make a Play-Doh wedding cake, in honor of Ms. Moffly and Mr. Bloom."

Sophie grinned. "You make the cake. I'll make the bride and groom to go on top!"

It was too bad there wasn't any *clean* dough left. Max had mixed all the colors up. But Sophie did the best she could. The bride's dress was a little pinkish. And the groom's tuxedo was blue. But Kate said that was just fine, since blue jeans were all that Mr. Bloom ever wore.

Sophie was working on a veil when she felt something soft brush her leg. She peeked under the table. "Tiptoe!" she said. It was her kitten's fluffy tail.

Sophie gently scooped her up and held the tiny Play-Doh veil over her ears. "Tiptoe would make a lovely bride! Don't you think, Kate?" she said.

Kate giggled. "Look out, Tiptoe. Sophie the Sweetheart's going to find a husband for you, too!"

Sophie grinned and set the kitten on the table so that she could sniff around. After a minute, Tiptoe made her way back to Sophie, jumped down, and curled up in her lap.

"Aw! You're so lucky," said Kate. "How come Tiptoe never picks me?"

"Well, I'm the one who feeds her," Sophie told Kate. She didn't want her friend to feel bad. But inside, she did feel very lucky. And not just because of Tiptoe.

She was also very lucky to have a friend like Kate. And a mom who said yes. And a big sister like Hayley—with great ideas, like dinner dates!

Just then, the phone rang. It was Kate's mom, saying it was time for Kate to go. Sophie made sure to be a sweetheart to Kate and let her cuddle Tiptoe before she walked home.

A few minutes later, Sophie's mom returned

with Max in her arms—kind of. He squirmed down and ran toward the table. *Ack!* Sophie whisked her Play-Doh bride and groom out of the way just in time.

"Sophie, will you be a sweetheart?" her mom asked.

Sophie grinned and raised her chin high. "That would be no problem at all!"

Her mom smiled. "Will you play with Max while I start dinner?"

Oh.

Sophie sighed.

"Yes, Mom."

"And make sure he doesn't eat any more Play-Doh. Okay?" her mom went on.

"Yes, Mom," Sophie repeated. Then she suddenly remembered Kate's Play-Doh cake!

She reached out to move it away from Max....

But she was too late.

Oops.

CHAPTER 3

The good news was Max did not throw up that night.

The better news was Sophie's mom called Ms. Moffly and Mr. Bloom to invite them to dinner on Friday. And both of them could come!

Sophie skipped all the way to the bus stop the next morning. She was so excited she couldn't stop. Plus it was a good way to keep up with Hayley so she could be *extra*-sweet to her!

Hayley had helped her so much with her great date idea. And Sophie wanted to say, "Thanks!"

But sweethearts didn't just use words, Sophie knew. They also did lots of sweet things!

She had already made Hayley's bed that morning. And picked out her clothes.

"What's this?" Hayley asked when she saw the shirt.

"I made it for you!" Sophie told her proudly. "Last night!"

Hayley was speechless for a second. "Why?" she said at last.

"Because you're the best sister in the whole world. And I want everyone to know. See? It says 'World's Number One Big Sister,' because that's exactly what you are!"

"Did you use my favorite shirt?" asked Hayley. She was touched. Sophie could tell.

Sophie crossed her arms proudly and grinned. "Yep, and my handy fabric markers! And glitter glue, of course!"

Hayley held up the shirt and stared at it. Sophie guessed she didn't know what to say about such an amazing gift. But that was fine. Sweethearts didn't need thank-yous.

"You are very welcome," Sophie said, anyway.

Still, she was a little surprised later, when Hayley headed to the bus stop—in a different shirt.

"Why aren't you wearing the shirt I made you?" Sophie asked as she skipped by her side.

Hayley shrugged. "Um...well...it's so nice," she said. "I don't want to mess it up."

A sweet feeling shot through Sophie, like she had warm maple syrup in her veins. "Oh, don't worry. I can always make you another one. In fact..." She got a great idea. "I can make a bunch!"

"No! Don't!" Hayley said quickly. "Really, Sophie, that's okay. One shirt is...*plenty*."

Sophie shrugged. "Whatever you say."

Then she noticed Hayley's backpack. Hey, that was another sweet thing she could do!

"Here!" Sophie yanked the strap off Hayley's

shoulder. "Let me carry that for you. And here!" She pulled a brush out of her own bag. "Let me fix your hair, too!"

"Sophie!" Hayley waved the brush away. "Everyone's staring—cut it out!"

Sophie looked ahead to the bus stop. A bunch of kids were already there. And yes, a bunch of them were staring. But let them stare at Sophie the Sweetheart helping the Number One Big Sister in the Whole World. *Big deal*, Sophie thought. *Who cares?*

Meanwhile, Hayley grabbed her backpack and hurried off to join her friends. Sophie sighed and sweetly called, "I love you, Hayley!"

Then Ella Fitzgibbon ran up to her, and Sophie sighed again.

Ella was in kindergarten. And yes, she was kind of cute. But Sophie thought she would be cuter if she weren't such a pest, too.

"Sophie! Guess what," Ella squealed.

"What, Ella?" Sophie said. (She would have ignored her if she weren't Sophie the

Sweetheart. But she couldn't do that now. Oh, well.)

Ella hopped up and down. "No!" she chirped. "You have to *guess*!"

Sophie crossed her arms. "Okay. Um . . . do you have to pee?" she asked.

Ella giggled. "No, silly Sophie! I peed at home! Guess again!"

You're moving to Alaska? Sophie smiled at the thought. But maybe that wasn't the sweetest answer. "I give up," she said. "What?"

"My mom had her baby!" Ella announced. "Now I'm a big sister, just like you!" Then she clapped her hands and spun around and around . . . until she got dizzy and fell down.

Sophie helped Ella up off the sidewalk. And she even tied her shoes. She had to admit, this was pretty big news.

Sophie remembered how excited she'd been two years earlier when Max was born. Then she remembered breakfast that morning and all the oatmeal Max had thrown. Sophie quickly felt her hair. Was there still some oatmeal there? Yep. There was.

"Congratulations," she told Ella. "I hope it's a girl."

☆   ☆   ☆

*W*oo! Sophie's ears were tired by the time she got to school. Ella's baby sister hadn't even come home from the hospital yet, and Ella still couldn't tell Sophie and Kate enough about her.

Sophie was glad to say good-bye—sweetly, of course. And glad to get to her classroom with Kate. And *very* glad when they saw Ms. Moffly.

"Good morning, girls," she greeted them.

"Good morning, Ms. Moffly!" said Sophie. "So can you really come over on Friday? You look nice today, by the way."

Ms. Moffly smoothed her hair. Her cheeks got pinker. "Why, thank you!" she said. "And yes. I'm looking forward to Friday. Your mom told me it was your idea." She turned to smile at Kate. "I'm so glad to hear you'll be there, too, Kate. It will be a night to remember, I bet."

Sophie looked at Kate and they shared a smile. Oh, if Ms. Moffly only knew!

They moved on to hang up their coats. "Here," Sophie said, reaching for Kate's. "Please. Allow me."

"Why, thank you, Sophie the Sweetheart!" Kate tossed her coat to her. "I think I'm going to like this name!"

"Hey, Sophie." Their friend Dean walked up just then. "Did I hear that Ms. Moffly's coming to your house?"

Sophie nodded. "You sure did."

Dean raised his eyebrows. *"Why?"*

"Yeah," said Jack, who was right behind him. His nose wrinkled up. "Ms. Moffly's nice and everything. But isn't seeing her in school enough?"

"Wait. Ms. Moffly's coming to your *house*?" Eve said. She and Mia were on Sophie's other side.

Sophie grinned. "I know it sounds a little weird. But wait till you hear the whole plan."

She waved them all in a little closer. But before she could explain, snooty Mindy VonBoffmann walked up and said in her snooty voice, "Sounds like Sophie wants to be the teacher's pet."

"Yeah," said Mindy's best friend, Lily Lemley. She always said "Yeah" to everything Mindy said.

Grrrr.

Sophie felt like growling. It was a feeling Mindy gave her a lot. She turned to Mindy, glaring. Then she remembered: She was Sophie the Sweetheart now!

She could not let Mindy get to her (like the old Sophie had).

She took a deep breath, closed her eyes, and let her glare melt away. By the time she opened her eyes, there was a sweet smile on her face.

"As a matter of fact, Mindy, I don't want to be the teacher's pet at all. All I want to be is a sweetheart." And she described her plan, right down to the wedding day, to everyone around.

"Who's Mr. Bloom again?" asked Jack.

"He rides that bike . . . ," Kate reminded him.

"Do you really think they'll invite us all to their wedding?" Eve chimed in.

Sophie shrugged. "Who else would they ask?"

Sophie could see her friends getting more and more excited. She could also see Mindy getting more and more mad. *Wait till I'm a flower girl!* she thought. She could just imagine Mindy's face then. But of course, she didn't say anything. A sweetheart would never rub it in.

At the same time, Sophie couldn't keep her smile from spreading from ear to ear. Sophie the Sweetheart was by far her best name yet!

CHAPTER 4

"Hi, Mr. Hurley!" said Sophie as she skipped into the gym later that morning. "I don't know what fun game you have planned for us. But I can't wait, whatever it is! See? I've got my shoelaces tied and everything. Nice shorts, by the way!"

"Er...thanks," said Mr. Hurley in a strange, normal voice. He almost even *smiled* as Sophie plopped down right in front of him, sitting crisscross applesauce.

Then he shook that look off and blew his whistle.

FWEEEEEEEEEEE!

"Okay, today we're starting a new unit! Everybody sit down and listen up!" This time, he hollered. That was mostly how he talked.

What kind of unit? Sophie wondered. Maybe gymnastics? That would be fun! Or soccer? Even better! Now that she was on a rec team, she could actually kick the ball!

Sophie was game for anything. (Just as long as it wasn't volleyball. The ball always seemed to fall on her head.)

Sophie listened, very sweetly, to what the gym teacher hollered next.

"Today we start square dancing!"

No! Not that!

"Ew!"

"Cooties!"

"Gross!"

All around her, kids started to gag. Sophie worked hard to keep smiling, though. She sat up nice and straight. And she didn't let out even a tiny groan.

FWEEEEEEEEEEE!

"Okay! That's enough!" Mr. Hurley hollered. "Not another word about germs!" He held up a pump bottle full of bright green gel. "I've got plenty of hand sanitizer for you all when you're done! Now I need two volunteers to demonstrate. Don't be shy! Hands up!"

Sophie looked around. Every hand was behind every back.

"If there aren't any volunteers, I'll pick!" Mr. Hurley warned.

Sophie looked around again. Now every head was looking at the floor.

Hey! Sophie suddenly thought of something sweet she could do right then. What did her mom always say? Something about turning lemons into lemonade? *Well,* Sophie thought, *maybe I can make some square-dance-ade today!*

She looked up, took a deep breath, and slowly raised her hand.

A giant *"Whuh!"* of surprise sucked half the air out of the gym.

"Okay, Sophie M. Get up here!" Mr. Hurley hollered.

Sophie got up and stood by his side. The girls in front of her sighed with relief. Kate was shaking her head in total disbelief.

"Now we need a boy!" Mr. Hurley hollered. "Who wants to join Sophie M.?"

Sophie bit her lip, and her eyes wandered. They landed hopefully on Ben. He was the nicest boy in her class, by far. Maybe he would be a sweetheart and raise his hand.

But no. He did not.

In fact, he didn't even look up. Instead, he picked at his jeans where there was already a hole.

Nobody else looked at Sophie, either. She was starting to feel sour instead of sweet. Why didn't anyone want to dance with her? What was so wrong? Did she stink?

"Okay! Looks like I'm picking. Let's see . . . Toby!" Mr. Hurley hollered. "Get up here!"

34

Sophie couldn't believe her ears.

Toby? No way!

Way.

Toby Myers was crossing his eyes and sticking out his tongue. "This is torture! Don't make me!" he moaned.

"On the double!" Mr. Hurley hollered.

Toby staggered to his feet, whining, "Why me?"

No, no, thought Sophie. *Why* me?

Why did Mr. Hurley have to pick the yuckiest boy in the whole school? Well, one of the yuckiest boys. There was also Yucky Boy Number Two—Archie Dolan, Toby's *new* best friend.

No one would ever know it now, but for a long time Sophie and Toby had been best friends. Toby would play at Sophie's house almost every day, or she would play at his. They had shared toys and costumes and everything. Even potties and juice boxes. *Blegh!*

But then something happened. When they

got to second grade, all of a sudden Toby started playing with Archie and calling Sophie names.

Luckily for Sophie, Kate moved to a house just down the street that year. It was like Sophie had written a letter to Santa asking for the perfect best friend. And Santa had decided she was so good that he gave her an early gift. Good old Kate!

At the front of the gym, Toby finally made his way to Sophie, but he leaned away as far as he could. Sophie started to lean away, too. Then she stopped herself.

Wait. No!

She wasn't going to let dumb Toby stop her from living up to her name. She was going to be Sophie the Sweetheart no matter what. No pain, no gain! (Just like her dad said when he went to the gym.)

She stood up very straight and smiled very, very big. "So, Mr. Hurley. What can we demonstrate for you today?" she asked sweetly.

Mr. Hurley got that funny look again—like his mouth was itching to grin. "Er . . . You can start by facing each other. No, Toby. The other way. Now 'honor your partner' with a big bow from the waist. Good, Sophie. Toby, try that again."

"*Ow!*"

Sophie grabbed the top of her head. Toby had bowed right into it! She stood up and almost, *almost* glared her maddest glare at him.

But then she remembered. She had to stay sweet, no matter what.

So instead, she rubbed her head and said, "Are you okay? How *clumsy* of me."

Boy, being sweet was hard! Especially when Toby do-si-doed all over her toes. And then when he swung her so hard by the arm that it almost came off!

She did get back at him, though. (In a sweet way, of course.) She grabbed his hands and held them—*tight!*—so he couldn't wriggle them away.

Take that, Toby!

"Okay, good job!" Mr. Hurley hollered at last. *Phew!*

Sophie sighed and rubbed her worn-out hands.

Mr. Hurley looked around the room. "Everyone else, stand up!"

After that, things began to get better. (They couldn't get much worse.) The whole class lined up to dance the Virginia reel. And it was actually kind of fun!

Sophie loved the sashay part. And the part where everybody ducked under the bridge. In fact, the only part she didn't like was the part where Mindy kept telling her what she was doing wrong.

"Sophie! Hold your hands higher!"

"Sophie! You're swinging wrong!"

"Sophie! You're sashaying too fast!"

"Sophie! Now you're sashaying too slow!"

Finally, Sophie turned to Mindy. She put her hands on her hips. "Stop telling me what to do!"

she snapped. "Mind your own beeswax, bossy-pants!"

"Ooooooh . . ."

The eyes all around them got big. Mindy's got bitter and small.

"I'm telling Mr. Hurley you called me a name!" she said.

A very un-sweet name, Sophie realized. *Uh-oh!*

"I'm sorry!" Sophie said quickly. "I didn't mean it! I take it back!"

Deep down, she didn't want to. But she knew a sweetheart could *not* talk like that. She hadn't let Toby ruin her name before. And she wasn't going to let Mindy ruin it now.

"I don't know what came over me," she told Mindy (and everybody else, since they were all listening, too). "It must be the square dancing. It brings out the worst in everyone."

She focused hard on smiling sweetly. There. Her cheeks hurt, so it must have worked.

"Please forgive me," she went on. "What I

really meant to say was thank you *so* much for all your helpful advice, Mindy. Those were *very* useful tips."

Mindy's eyes opened a little. "You're welcome," she said curtly.

"So we're good?" Sophie asked.

Mindy straightened her headband. "Yeah. For now, I guess."

☆　☆　☆

Sophie spent the rest of the school day being extra-sweet to everyone. But she couldn't help wondering: Was it enough?

Had she made up for snapping at Mindy? And calling her a name?

On the bus home from school, she asked Kate what she thought. (That was after she brushed off the best seat for Hayley and gave her the pudding cup she'd saved from lunch.)

"Oh, for sure," Kate told her. "When you sharpened everyone's pencils? That was sweet! And when you asked the lunch ladies for their *delicious* meat loaf recipe? Remember? They

41

were so happy they almost cried." She waggled her eyebrows. "Just stay away from Mindy from now on. Then it'll be easy to be a sweetheart!"

Kate's right! Sophie thought.

But by the time she got home, she thought again...

Hmm...

What if the best way to prove she was a sweetheart was to stay *close* to Mindy...or even act like her friend!

CHAPTER 5

"Good morning, Mindy!" Sophie sang out cheerfully. Mindy had just walked through the classroom door. It was Wednesday—or Be-Extra-Sweet-to-Mindy Day, as Sophie would call it from now on.

"Good morning," grumbled Mindy. She lifted her pointy chin so she could look down her pointy nose.

Ugh! A little voice spoke up in Sophie's head. "It's not worth it! Pick another name!" it warned.

But then another voice said, "You can do this.

Don't give up." And since it was just a little louder, Sophie listened to that one.

She looked right back at Mindy. "That's a really nice headband," she said.

Mindy pulled her headband forward, then pushed it back again. "I know. You should try one sometime." She went on. "A brush might help, too."

With that, she strutted off. Sophie forced a grin and watched her go.

"Okay, Mindy!" she called. "That's great advice. Thank you!"

Eve, who was standing next to her, clearly could not believe her ears or eyes. "Sophie! How can you be so nice when she says stuff like that?" she asked.

Sophie clasped her hands and sighed. "Because I'm a sweetheart," she replied.

"I don't get it," Mia said, joining them. "Remember how she dared you to take that gift from my birthday party? I'm still so mad at her for that. Why aren't you?"

Sophie shrugged. Oh, she was still mad at Mindy. And she probably would be for the rest of her life. But right now, being Sophie the Sweetheart was a lot more important.

She could tell that Eve and Mia were impressed. Now she hoped they'd tell everyone else! In the meantime, Sophie had to find more ways to be nice to the meanest girl in the class.

Unfortunately, she couldn't hang up Mindy's jacket. Or turn in her homework for her. Lily already did those things (and many, many more) for Mindy.

But as soon as Ms. Moffly took attendance, Sophie realized something.

"Lily Lemley?" the teacher called.

No answer.

Aha!

Lily was absent! Maybe Sophie would have more chances to be sweet to Mindy that day after all.

She was determined to take every chance she could get.

"Here, Mindy. I'll toss that trash for you," she said after snack.

"Why?" Mindy frowned.

"Why not?" Sophie smiled back.

Later it was time for workstations. That was when the class broke into pairs and picked from things Ms. Moffly called Enriching Activities. Sophie wasn't sure exactly why she called them that. Yes, they were activities, like writing about pictures and doing science experiments. But they sure hadn't made Sophie rich at all.

They were supposed to try different subjects each time. And different partners, too. Mindy and Lily always seemed to forget that part. But now that Lily was absent...

"Would you like to be my partner?" Sophie asked Mindy.

"I guess so." Mindy shrugged.

"Great!" Sophie grinned.

Wow. She'd kind of thought Mindy might make a face and say no.

Sophie looked around. "So...want to do Math Games?" That was her favorite activity.

But Mindy crossed her arms. "We're doing Computers. I can't stand Math Games."

Fine, Sophie grumbled inside. But outside, she smiled and said, "Okay!"

Of course, Sophie knew if they picked Computers, they would have to share a laptop. And Sophie knew what *that* would mean. Mindy would hog the keyboard the whole time.

And Sophie was right.

Still. She stayed sweet—on the outside.

But on the inside, she was boiling up. By lunchtime, she needed a break. Sophie was happy to sit down with Kate, someone she didn't have to work to be sweet to!

Then she noticed Mindy coming out of the lunch line—alone. She was holding her tray and looking around. Sophie guessed she wasn't used to lunch without Lily. Who would find a chair for her and pull it out?

Hmm.

Sophie's mind started cranking. Maybe this was another chance to be sweet! Should she take it? She didn't really want to. But then what kind of sweetheart would she be?

"Hey, Kate," she finally whispered. "Watch this." Then she waved and raised her voice. She wanted to be sure the whole class heard her call, "Hey, Mindy! Want to sit with us?"

"What are you doing?" Kate's eyes asked her.

"Don't worry," Sophie's smile said back. She knew Mindy wouldn't come over. Mindy never sat with them.

But to her surprise — and Kate's — this time she *did*.

Mindy walked right up. She sat right down. And she started to eat her turkey dog.

"What are *you* staring at?" asked Mindy. That was when Sophie realized her jaw had dropped.

At you, she thought. *Sitting here with us. And not even telling us how to eat.*

"Uh...nothing," she said out loud. "How's your turkey dog, Mindy?"

☆　☆　☆

After lunch came recess. And by then, Sophie the Sweetheart was on a roll.

"I can't believe you cleared Mindy's tray for her," Kate said as they walked outside.

Sophie nodded, grinning. "I know. Neither can I! But if I can be that sweet to Mindy, I'm a sweetheart for sure!"

Mindy was already out on the blacktop with Sydney and Grace and the other Sophie in their class, Sophie A. Sophie and Kate usually played other games, but these girls jumped rope every day. And every day, they started with the same old debate about who got to jump first and who had to turn the rope.

"Hey, Kate," Sophie said. "How about we jump rope today?"

"Okay, sure. But why?"

"Because I just thought of another job for Sophie the Sweetheart," Sophie whispered back.

They hurried to the jump-rope corner, where

Sophie promptly took the rope from Mindy's hand.

"Hey! What are you doing?" snapped Mindy.

"I'm turning the rope for you!" Sophie said.

She turned the rope the *whole* time. She didn't even jump. Not once! Every time her turn came up, she let another girl go for her.

"Are you sure you don't want to jump?" asked Sydney after several rounds.

Mindy answered for her. "You heard her say she didn't, which means it's my turn now."

She stepped up to the rope and Sophie started turning again. Sophie A. held the other end.

"Higher!" Mindy ordered.

"I'm trying," Sophie told her. And really, she was. But her arm was so heavy and sore now, she could hardly lift it up. It was really starting to burn, like a thousand tiny dragons were inside, breathing fire.

Finally, Mindy jumped in.

"*Teddy Bear, Teddy Bear,*" everyone started to sing.

But before they got any further, the rope tripped Mindy—*"Ooph!"*—and she fell to her knees.

"You did that on purpose!" shouted Mindy.

"But I didn't!" Sophie said. She couldn't let her name be ruined by an accident like this! "My arm just got so tired," she explained. "I'm really sorry! I didn't mean to. I swear!"

Kate spoke up. "Sophie would never do that on purpose."

Sophie A. joined her. "It was just an accident, Mindy. Relax."

Sophie gave them both a grateful smile. But Mindy still looked very mad. In fact, her face was as red as a rubber kickball—the kind that came zooming in just then!

"Look out!" called Dean from across the blacktop.

But it was too late. The ball hit Mindy— *smack!*—in her pinchy, sour face. It must have hit her hard, too. Dean had kicked the ball, and he was the biggest kid in their grade.

Mindy went flying back instantly as the ball bounced off her nose and hopped happily away.

"Ah!" Mindy yelled, covering her face.

"Sorry!" Dean called.

The other kickball players, meanwhile, had started to laugh. Soon the basketball players and tag players were laughing, too. Only the jump-ropers weren't. They were standing with their hands over their big, round mouths. Sophie bet if they took their hands away too fast, their own laughs would spill out.

But Sophie decided something: Sweethearts didn't laugh; they helped. Besides, Mindy had been kneeling there because of her. And it looked like she was really hurt!

"Are you okay?" Sophie asked Mindy. She bent down and gently helped her sit up.

Mindy's shoulders trembled. Her head shook from side to side. Slowly, she let her hands down. Her face was all different colors of red now. And her eyes were wet. Stuff was even starting to spill out! Wait. Was Mindy *crying*?

Sophie had seen Mindy cry before. Everybody had. But it was always pretty . . . well, *fake*. There were never any real tears.

"Where does it hurt?" Sophie asked her.

Mindy sniffled and held up her hand. There was a tiny scrape on her palm. *That must hurt a lot more than it looks like it does*, Sophie thought. *Or maybe*, she realized suddenly, *something else hurts even more*.

By then, Ms. Moffly was outside with them. Recess was over. It was time to go in.

"What happened?" she asked, hurrying over.

"Mindy tripped on the jump rope. *Accidentally*," said Sophie. "And then Dean went and hit her in the head."

"Dean *what*?" Ms. Moffly gasped.

"With the ball, I mean," Sophie said. "And it was probably an accident, too. Don't worry. Nobody can aim a kickball that well."

"Do you need to go to the nurse, Mindy?" Ms. Moffly asked. She knelt so they were nose-to-nose.

Mindy sniffled—twice this time—and nodded.

"Oh, I can take her," Sophie offered. "I know the way by heart."

Ms. Moffly smiled. "Yes, I guess you do by now. That's very sweet, Sophie. Thank you."

Wow! Sophie didn't know what was sweeter—her or the way she felt!

She took Mindy's hand and led her inside, up the stairs. "Does it hurt a lot?" Sophie asked. "I just want to warn you, it'll hurt even more when Mrs. Frost rubs that sting-y stuff on it."

Mindy stopped and turned to Sophie. Her tears were finally drying up. She still looked sad, but not so splotchy. And not snooty at all. For once. "I hate that sting-y stuff!" She gulped.

"I know." Sophie nodded. "Me too. But sometimes it helps to hold someone's hand when she puts it on. If you want, you can hold mine."

"That would help a lot," Mindy said.

Then she sniffed again and made a face Sophie wasn't used to (on Mindy, at least). A smile. "You really didn't trip me?"

"No way!" Sophie said.

"I thought maybe you were still mad at me . . . about that dare. You know, taking Mia's present at her party. I'm sorry about that."

Mindy was sorry? Without an I'm-not-*really*-sorry face? That surprised Sophie, too!

"Uh . . . it's okay. I got over it," said Sophie.

"You know, nobody but Lily is ever this nice to me," Mindy confessed. "It's kind of nice to have another friend."

Mindy's *friend*? Sophie heard the word, but it took a minute to sink in. Was that really what she was now? That hadn't been her plan. And yet here they were, sharing smiles and holding hands.

Before she could say or do anything else, the nurse's door opened wide.

"Well, well, well, Sophie Miller," said the nurse, Mrs. Frost. "What in the world have you done to yourself now?"

"Oh, it's not me, Mrs. Frost," Sophie said quickly. "It's Mindy, here. My friend."

CHAPTER 6

Sophie couldn't believe it. Being sweet to Mindy had gone so well! In fact, she didn't even have to *try* to be sweet anymore that day. It just happened. By itself.

Mindy smiled at Sophie when it was time to go home. And the next morning, when they got to school, she waved and said hello.

"Hi!" Sophie said back, giving Mindy a big smile. "So, how's your hand?"

"It's okay." Mindy showed off a big pink bandage. It was sparkly!

Cool!

"Where did you get that?" Sophie asked.

"On the Internet," Mindy explained. "I'll have my mom order some for you."

Suddenly, Lily ran up and hugged Mindy. "I'm back! I was sick, but I'm all better now!" Then she turned to Sophie. "What are *you* doing here?" her eyes asked.

Lily started to say something. Probably "Get lost," Sophie guessed.

But Mindy stopped her. "It's okay."

Lily turned back to see if she'd heard right. "It *is*?"

Mindy nodded. "Sure. We're all friends."

Sophie watched the idea hit Lily. She seemed as surprised as Sophie had been.

"But you can still hang up my coat, Lily," Mindy told her. She slipped her jacket off. "Here."

She waved to Sophie as they walked off. Sophie waved back to her and grinned.

Then—*"Ooph!"*—Sophie suddenly stumbled forward.

Hey! What was that?

"Out of my way!" Toby said, shoving past.

"Hey! Watch where you're going!" Sophie began to shout.

But then she stopped. Sophie the Sweetheart couldn't say that.

"Excuse me!" she called instead, sweetly. "I'm so sorry if I was in your way!"

Then a thought hit her—*whomp!*—in the very front of her brain.

Being a sweetheart to Mindy had gone way better than planned. But Mindy wasn't the only hard-to-be-sweet-to kid in her class. Sophie could almost hear the other kids saying, "Wow! Can you believe how sweet Sophie is to Mindy? And *Toby*, too?"

And better yet, if she listened hard, she could almost hear Toby saying something, as well. Something like "I forgot how nice you were, Sophie. Do you want to be friends again?"

She couldn't wait to tell Kate her latest and greatest idea!

But when she did, Kate just looked worried. "Are you sure you can do this, Sophie?" she asked. "I mean, I know you said Mindy might have some good qualities. But Toby? I don't know. Plus, how sweet can you be to him when his face makes you sick?"

"Not his whole face," Sophie said, correcting her. *Just all those freckles, and that ketchup hair, and those big beaver teeth.* "And he doesn't make me sick, exactly." *Just a little ill sometimes.* "If I'm going to be a real sweetheart, I'm going to have to try my best with everyone. Even Toby."

It was Thursday, which meant they had gym again. And that meant square dancing. Again. But this was a great chance to be sweet to Toby—one that Sophie couldn't miss!

This time, Mr. Hurley let them pick their own partners if they wanted to.

Sophie raised her hand. She was the only one. "I pick Toby," she declared.

"You do?!" Toby's face got red. Even redder than his hair.

"*Mmm-hmm.*" Sophie smiled sweetly and nodded. But suddenly, what she really wanted to do was run out of the gym.

She should have known better. She should have known Toby would act like he had before: like he'd rather be getting a shot in the arm than square dancing with her.

At first, Sophie tried to ignore him. But she was a sweetheart, not a saint. Then she realized there was another way to be sweet to Toby.

"You know what, Mr. Hurley?" she said loudly. "I think I changed my mind. This seems to make Toby very unhappy, and I would hate to do that. I'd like to pick Ben instead. If that's okay with you and Ben, of course."

Ben shrugged and fixed his glasses. "Sure," he said. "Okay with me."

Mr. Hurley scratched his head with his whistle. "Uh, yeah. Sounds good, I think."

Sophie turned to Toby. "Never mind," she sweetly said.

Toby looked surprised, like he'd gotten the

shot and it hadn't hurt a bit. It wasn't exactly a look that said, "You're a sweetheart." *But that's okay*, thought Sophie. She was just warming up.

☆ ☆ ☆

All day long, Sophie looked for another way to be sweet to Toby. She found her next chance in art class. Ms. Bart, the art teacher, had asked them each to make a flag on a piece of paper. She told them all, "It should represent *you*!"

Toby made a big blue star on his flag. Of course, Sophie knew why. It was the logo of his favorite football team, the Dallas Cowboys. It would have been very easy for the old Sophie to say something not-so-sweet to him then. Something like "That doesn't represent you, Toby. It represents a football team."

But Sophie the Sweetheart would never say that! What she did say was "I like your flag a lot. You did a really good job with your star."

"Uh, thanks." Toby looked up. His eyes zipped back and forth. He checked to make

62

sure she was talking about *his* flag. Yep. It was the only one with a big star.

Sophie went on. "You should keep it, for when you make the team one day."

Toby checked again to make sure she wasn't teasing him. So Sophie made her most sincere, no-way-am-I-teasing-you face.

He nodded to the giant red heart on her paper. "Your flag's nice, too," he said—so softly she almost didn't hear.

Sophie grinned. Yes, it *was* nice. She'd worked hard on it. (Heart shapes were not easy!) But Sophie was smiling for another reason, too. That was the first compliment Toby had given her in a very long time.

"Thanks," she said back. And this time, she and Toby shared a smile. In fact, Sophie looked at Toby's face for a whole second before she realized she didn't feel the teeniest bit ill. It was almost like the old days, when they had looked at each other and felt like friends.

"So, how are your cats doing?" she asked

Toby. "You should meet my kitten, Tiptoe, sometime."

"Cool. Maybe," said Toby. "When'd you get her? What's she like?"

Sophie leaned forward. She was just about to tell him how cuddly and *sweet* Tiptoe was when all of a sudden a hand grabbed the edge of her flag and started to tug.

"Hey! My heart!" Sophie cried. She followed the hand . . . to the arm . . . all the way up . . . to Archie's face!

He pulled the flag toward him. "So, what's this? A big valentine?" He was grinning like a shark.

"No!" Sophie said in what she hoped was a sweet voice. "It's my flag. So *please* get your hands off!"

She tried to pull her flag back—but that was a mistake. Archie held on tight. And Sophie's heart began to break.

Rrrriiiip!

"You tore my flag!" cried Sophie.

"Ha!" Archie laughed. "It wasn't my fault.

You're the one that pulled." Then he turned to Toby. "You saw her, right?"

Ugh! Sophie looked down and gritted her teeth and waited for Toby to say, "Yeah." She waited for him to take Archie's side and laugh — and make everything even worse.

It was going to be very hard to be sweet then. She might even have to give up her name.

But Toby didn't say, "Yeah," at all. He said something else.

"Why did you do that?" he asked Archie. "She wasn't bothering you."

"What do you care?" said Archie. "Is she your *girlfriend* now? *Oooh!*"

"No!" Toby shot back.

Sophie sighed. *Here it comes.* Now *he'll turn on me for sure,* she thought.

But to her surprise, Toby didn't. What he did do was make his eyes very small. "You're such a jerk-face, Archie!" he said.

Jerk-face?

Sweet! Sophie thought.

CHAPTER 7

$\mathcal{N}$obody could believe it. Especially Sophie.

Toby and Archie were in a fight! They weren't talking. They weren't even looking at each other. Room 10 had never been as quiet as it was after art.

"I have to commend you on your behavior," Ms. Moffly said happily as she sent the class to lunch. "You all might just earn extra free time this week, if you keep up the good work."

Sophie was still mad about her heart flag, of course. She hadn't had time to make another one. Ms. Bart had helped her tape it instead. At the same time, some good things had come out of her broken heart.

"I can't believe you were so sweet about the whole thing," lots of kids had said.

"What can I say?" Sophie had told them. "Just call me Sophie the Sweetheart!"

It helped a lot to know that Toby had taken her side. (And that Archie would be cleaning paintbrushes for the rest of his life!)

Sophie walked out of the lunch line with Kate, feeling just about as sweet as could be.

"Hi, Sophie." Mindy waved to her. "Do you want to sit with us?"

Sophie turned to Kate, who shrugged. But then another table caught her eye. It was the far one, where Toby was sitting by himself.

Poor Toby. He looked like he'd lost his best friend—which he kind of had.

"Sorry, Mindy. I can't. But thanks a lot," she said. Then she nodded for Kate to follow her.

"We're sitting with Toby? Really?" Kate's mouth dropped open.

"I have to," Sophie whispered. "I'm Sophie the Sweetheart. And remember, he stood up for me in art."

"Hi, Toby. Mind if we sit here?" Sophie plunked down her tray.

Toby stared at her. Sophie tried to read his face. It kind of said, "What are you doing here?" But it didn't say, "Go away."

So she took the seat next to Toby. Kate took the one next to her.

This is even weirder than lunch with Mindy, Sophie thought.

"So." Sophie sighed happily. She smiled at Toby, then at Kate. "What should we talk about? Ms. Moffly and Mr. Bloom's big date?"

"Of course!" Kate nodded eagerly. "It's tomorrow! I'm so excited!"

"Me too!" Sophie grinned.

They both turned to Toby to hear his "Me three!" But all he did was chug his milk and burp. Then he jammed a taco into his mouth.

"Uh...so...what do you think?" Sophie

went on. "What kind of wedding should they have? Big and fancy, like a royal wedding? Or outside, like my mom's cousin had, with sunglasses and bare feet?"

"Definitely royal," said Kate.

Sophie nodded. "I agree."

Finally, Toby swallowed and shrugged. "I don't know. I hate wearing church shoes. So outside sounds pretty good to me, I guess."

☆　　☆　　☆

Toby didn't say much more at lunch. He just ate and cleared his tray, then went outside for recess all by himself. He was still all by himself a few minutes later, when Sophie headed out with Kate.

Usually, Toby played basketball at recess. But Archie was already on the court. Toby looked like he wanted to go out there, too—until Archie shot him a long, hard look.

Poor Toby, Sophie thought. *Good thing he has Sophie the Sweetheart around!*

Sophie knew how it was hard to lose a friend. Even a friend like Archie. (Yuck.)

She dragged Kate over to Toby, grinning. "Forget about Archie!" she said. "You can play with us! It'll be fun. Right, Kate?"

She smiled at Kate. But Kate didn't really smile back. Instead, she crossed her arms.

"But I thought we were going to play *our* game," Kate said in a low voice.

Sophie nodded. "I know. And Toby can play, too. Come on!" she said, turning back to him. "It's way more fun than basketball."

Toby frowned as if that were impossible. "How do you play?"

"You just play," Sophie explained. "Remember when we were little? How you used to pretend you were a superhero? And I was a talking horse? Well, it's like that . . . except way more grown up, of course. I'm an international super-spy. And Kate's a wild animal emergency vet."

"Do you want to be a sick animal?" Kate asked him. "We could rescue you and operate."

"No." Toby crossed his arms and made a "what are you talking about?" face.

He didn't want to be a superhero, either.

Or a flying robot, believe it or not.

"Well, what do you want to be?" Sophie finally asked him. Playing with him in kindergarten had never been this hard!

"I don't know." Toby kicked a pebble. "Why can't I just be me?"

"Because that's no fun!" said Sophie. She almost rolled her eyes. But since that wasn't a sweet thing to do, she just sighed. "Okay. Be yourself."

But the game wasn't the same. Sophie wasn't sure any of them had fun. And she wasn't even sure she was cheering Toby up that much.

Before long, he said, "I think I'll go play basketball."

But almost as soon as he said that, Archie yelled over, "Having fun with your *girlfriend*, Toby? Is she your *sweetheart* now, or what?"

Grrr! Sophie didn't know who was madder,

Toby or her. Toby was a lot redder, that was for sure. But Sophie was steaming inside. It was hard to be sweet. She had to close her eyes and bite her lip and squeeze her fists.

Finally, Sophie opened her eyes and took a deep breath. "Who cares what he says, anyway?" she told Toby. "He's just a jerk-face, right?"

But Toby didn't say anything back. Sophie looked around. He wasn't there!

"Where'd he go?" she asked Kate.

Kate nodded to the big school doors.

He ran inside? Sophie sighed. She guessed *Toby* cared what Archie thought. Or maybe he just had to pee. (But somehow, she doubted that.)

It looked like Sophie would have to be even sweeter to Toby now. So sweet that it made up for Archie's big fat mouth. But she also had to be careful. She wanted to be *a* sweetheart. But not *Toby's* sweetheart, or anything lovey-dovey like that. Gross!

So what could she do? *Hmm.* She didn't know.

But Hayley was an expert in boy stuff. Sophie would ask her for advice on the bus!

Sophie couldn't wait for school to be over. She hurried to the bus as soon as Ms. Moffly let them go. But Hayley wasn't there. Had she gone home sick? Sophie hoped not. Especially after she'd brought Hayley that nice orange that morning. And peeled it for her at the bus stop, too. And told Sam, "Get away from my sister!" when he started to sneeze all over it. Ew!

But when Sophie got home, her mom said Hayley was fine. *Hooray!*

She ran upstairs and found Hayley reading in their room.

"Hayley!" she cried, hugging her. "I missed you! Why weren't you on the bus?"

Hayley sighed and hugged her back. "Kim's mom was picking her up," she explained. "So I asked her to bring me home, too."

"Oh, okay." Sophie gave her one more tight squeeze. Then she hopped up on her bed. "I have to ask you something!"

But before she could, Hayley closed her book. "I didn't *want* to ride the bus," she said.

"Okay." Sophie shrugged. She didn't always want to ride the bus, either, she guessed. "Now, here's my question—"

"Hang on, Sophie." Hayley stopped her. "Don't you want to know why?"

Sophie shrugged again. "Because Kim's mom has that cool van? Hey! Do you think Kate and I could get a ride with you guys next time?"

Hayley bit her lip. "That's the thing, Sophie. *That's* why I didn't ride the bus."

Huh?

"You've been all over me this week, Sophie. And, well, it's just too much."

Too much?

What was Hayley saying?

"I'm just trying to be sweet," Sophie explained. "And show everyone what a great sister you are. Don't you want them all to know?"

Hayley sighed and shook her head. "Honestly? No."

Then she sat down next to Sophie. "Look. I know you're just being sweet, Sophie. But it's embarrassing in front of my friends. I know that you love me. And I love you, too. But you know what the sweetest thing you could do for me is?"

Sophie shrugged. She couldn't imagine. She thought she'd done everything she could.

Hayley put her arm around her shoulder. "Leave me alone."

Sophie looked up at her sister. *Really?* She watched Hayley smile.

"It's kind of like Ella," Hayley went on gently. "And how she drives you so crazy, you always say."

Oh, no!

"I'm not that bad!" Sophie swallowed hard. "Am I?"

Hayley patted her back. "No . . . but almost."

"I am so sorry!" Sophie hung her head. "I'll never talk to you again."

Hayley laughed. "That's not what I'm saying.

I know you're just being nice. Just like Ella's trying to be. But if you could talk to me like you used to, that would be really great. Besides, it's not like I'm asking you to stop making my bed or anything."

Sophie smiled.

"Just kidding," said Hayley, winking. "So, what did you want to ask me?"

Oh, right! Sophie had almost forgotten. How to help Toby. Of course.

She started to tell Hayley everything. But then she stopped. *Hang on!* Maybe Hayley had already answered her question in a way....

"You know what? Nothing! Never mind. You really are the World's Number One Big Sister! Hey—" Sophie suddenly got another idea. She was so full of them that day! "If you're not going to wear that shirt I made you...could I have it back, Hayley?"

CHAPTER 8

The next day was Friday—the Big Teacher-Date Day. At last! But that wasn't all Sophie was thinking about. She had some more important Sophie the Sweetheart work to do.

"Guess what! My sister came home from the hospital!" cried Ella, running up to her at the bus stop. "And guess what! She brought my mom!"

"Are they making you wash your hands a lot?" Sophie asked her.

Ella nodded hard. "Uh-huh!"

"So . . . where's your shirt?" asked Sophie.

Ella looked down and opened her coat. "Right here on my tummy, silly." She grinned. "Same place as yours."

"I mean, where's your official *big sister* shirt?" Sophie crossed her arms and watched as Ella's eyes got very big.

"I don't know!" Ella said. "Where do you get them?"

That was when Sophie uncrossed her arms, unzipped her bag, and reached inside. She pulled out the shirt she'd made for Hayley and held it up. "Ta-da!"

"Oh!" Ella gasped. "It's beautiful! Is it for *me*?"

"Are you the World's Number One Big Sister?" asked Sophie.

Ella nodded eagerly. She quickly slipped off her jacket and put the shirt on over her regular clothes. It came almost down to her knees. But Ella didn't mind at all.

"I love it!" Ella cried. She began to twirl around. "Thank you, Sophie! I'm never, ever, ever going to take it off!"

A feeling wrapped up Sophie — as if invisible arms were hugging her, tight. She laughed. It had to be the sweetest feeling in the world!

But then Sophie noticed Hayley, around the corner with her friends. She was looking at Sophie and Ella...and smiling at them. Sophie was wrong, she suddenly realized. There *was* a sweeter feeling. And she was feeling it right then.

The sweet feeling lasted through the whole bus ride, all the way to school.

And then it was time for Sophie to do Sweet Thing Number Two.

"Move it," said Sophie, walking up behind Toby in the classroom. "Do you mind? You're in my way."

"Huh?" Toby was putting his homework in the Homework Basket. He spun around to look at Sophie in surprise. "Er...sorry. Okay."

He stepped aside, and Sophie rolled her eyes. "You should be," she said. "Sheesh!"

Then she peeked over her shoulder to make sure that Archie had seen.

He had. And he was staring. So was everybody else.

Even Kate's mouth had dropped open. She
grabbed Sophie's hand and pulled her close.
"What happened to being a *sweetheart*?" she
whispered.

Sophie just shrugged and squeezed her hand.
If she could have winked, she would have done
that to Kate, as well.

Because she *was* being a sweetheart — even
though it didn't look like that. It was all part
of her super-sweet Help-Cheer-Up-Toby
Plan.

After all, she had a feeling that Toby wanted
to make up with Archie but didn't know how.
And the sweetest thing Sophie could do was try
to help him out. All she had to do, she figured,
was start a nice, big fight — and hope that
Archie would butt in and take Toby's side.

But how should she start it? Sophie looked
around.

She could punch him, she guessed.

But no. That was *too* mean. (And what if he punched her back?)

Wait! I know! she thought suddenly. It came to her in a flash. She grabbed a piece of paper, ran to her table, and wrote something down fast.

After a minute, Sophie leaned back and looked at her work. A masterpiece!

She wrote her name and dotted the *i* with a great big heart.

There! All done!

She ran up to Dean and gave him the paper. "Here," she said. "Pass this around. Before the bell rings."

Dean read it.

The cowboys are the wurst team in the world!!!!
   Sophie the Sweetheart
   XXXOOO

"Really?" he asked.

Sophie grinned. "Go ahead!" She pointed to

Toby, who was just sitting down. "In fact, why don't you start with him?"

Not a minute later, Toby ran up to her desk. He held the paper in front of her nose. "Did you really write this, Sophie?" he snapped.

"That's my signature, all right," she said.

Toby frowned a big frown. "Well, you'd better take it back!"

Sophie smiled *sweetly*. "I will not."

That was when Archie stomped up, fuming. "Does that say what I think it does?" He read the note over Toby's shoulder. "You are so asking for it!" he growled at Sophie.

"I know! Right?" Toby glared.

Then Toby turned to Archie. And Archie turned to him. "The Cowboys rule!" they said together. They bumped fists and shared a smile.

Yes! Sophie's plan had worked. Toby and Archie weren't in a fight anymore! Inside, she patted herself on the back.

Then both boys turned back to her. They weren't smiling anymore.

Uh-oh.

Sophie stepped back. She hadn't planned this far. What exactly was she going to do now?

Lucky for her — *Brrriiinnnng!!!!* — the bell rang. *Phew!*

She had never been so happy for school to start.

☆   ☆   ☆

Sophie's plan worked! By lunchtime, Toby and Archie were sitting together again, flicking peas with their spoons. She just wished they weren't flicking every pea at her.

Still, she felt as sweet as ever. By being mean to Toby, she had clearly helped him a lot. And wasn't that really, deep down, what being a sweetheart was all about?

Plus Kate was happy, too. "I'm glad it's just us again," she said at lunch. She picked a pea out of Sophie's hair. "For you!" She held it out.

"Thanks." Sophie squished it between her fingers. "And yeah. I know what you mean." She wrinkled her nose and nodded to Toby.

"Trust me, when I decided to be sweet, I never planned on eating with him."

Of course, now she had another problem. People weren't calling her a sweetheart anymore. (At least, not the Cowboys fans. Who knew there were so many in school?)

Oh, well. Sophie would worry about that later. She had bigger things to think about now. It was finally Friday, Ms. Moffly and Mr. Bloom's Big Date Night! Very soon they'd be in love. And then, thanks to Sophie, *they'd* be sweethearts. And Sophie wouldn't be surprised if when they got married they made her Flower Girl Number *One*!

CHAPTER 9

Everything was perfect. Sophie was so excited when she got home from school! She had run ahead of Hayley, who was walking *slowly* with her friends.

Mmm! Her mom was making lasagna. Sophie could tell by the warm, happy smell.

And the house looked so neat! Where had her mom hidden all their junk?

Sophie found her mom in the kitchen and gave her a big sweetheart hug. Then she ran up to her room to hurry to change clothes.

She and Kate had already decided to dress up

for dinner. They had to wear something that said "special date." And "Wouldn't I make a great flower girl?"

Unfortunately, Sophie didn't have anything that said exactly that. In fact, the only thing her dresses said was "Handmade by Grandma Hamm."

At last, she picked out the red one. Red was the color of *love*, after all. But it needed something more. Accessories!

Let's see. . . .

Sophie put on her favorite necklace, the one with the cat with the sparkly eyes. Sophie was pretty sure they were real diamonds, so she wore it only at special times.

Then she spotted the ladybug brooch from her Great-aunt Maggie. *Perfect!* She pinned it on.

And the ring from Mia's party goody bag.

And the glow-in-the-dark bracelets she had won at the school fair. (She had set a school record at the ringtoss!)

Then Sophie looked in the mirror and practiced some smiles. And some "Who? Me? I'd love to be your flower girl!" faces, making sure to look surprised.

"What are you doing?"

Sophie turned. Hayley was standing in the doorway.

"Nothing," Sophie said. "Just getting ready for tonight."

"Did Mom say we had to dress up?" Hayley asked.

Sophie struck a very fancy pose. "No. I just thought it would be nice."

Hayley grinned. "Well, if you're going to wear that, I think you need your hair up. Don't you?" She picked up her brush and her box of bobby pins.

"You're the best!" Sophie cried. "But don't worry," she quickly added. "I won't tell anyone."

☆   ☆   ☆

A little later, Sophie hurried back to the kitchen with her hair up in a tight bun. She looked just like the girl in Hayley's ballet poster, except she had bangs and that girl did not.

By then, her dad was home. He was fixing a salad in the big wooden bowl. "Wow!" he said as soon as he saw her. "Sophie, sweetheart, is that you?"

Sophie smiled and straightened the earrings she'd found in her old Pretty Princess game. "Of course it's me, Dad! Is anybody else here yet?" She looked at the clock.

"No, sweetie. Relax. We still have an hour," answered her mom.

Sophie groaned. A whole hour! Sixty minutes! How could she ever wait that long?

"Hey, Sophie, I have an idea," her mom said. She nodded to Max. He was standing by the watercooler, turning the water on and off. "Why don't you take Max outside before we have a flood?"

"Mom." Sophie held out her skirt. "I can't take Max outside like *this*."

Her mom smiled. "I guess you're right. Maybe

I can get Hayley to play with him. How about you set the table, then? Everything's in the dining room, all ready to put out."

"Great!" Sophie skipped into the dining room. She loved eating in there. It was a pretty funny name, though, for a room they dined in only a few times a year.

Her mom had already laid out a tablecloth—the white one with the lace trim. Sophie carefully picked up the clinky good plates and set them out, one at a time.

Then she moved on to the silverware. Did forks go on the left? *Hmm.* The right?

Oh, I'll do them both ways, Sophie finally decided. Then at least only half would be wrong.

There! she thought when the last place was set and all the napkins were folded into fans. (She had learned that trick from the nice waiter at the Chinese restaurant in town.)

But something was missing.

Candles! Of course. Every dinner date needed a bunch of those!

Sophie dashed back into the kitchen, calling, "Mom! Dad!" But her parents weren't there. So Sophie went ahead and poked around. There had to be candles somewhere.

All she could find were birthday candles. *Well, they're better than nothing,* she thought.

What could she put them in? Not the big candlesticks. (She tried. It didn't work.)

Think! Sophie told herself.

Then she remembered Max's Play-Doh in the cabinet and ran to pull it out.

She took some purplish dough and squished it down until she had a big, flat heart. Then she stuck all twelve birthday candles in and put it in the middle of the big table. *Ta-da!*

Much better! she thought. *Now, I'll sit here, and Ms. Moffly will sit there, and Mr. Bloom will sit there and ... huh?*

Wait. Sophie counted the places. Why were there eight?

Sophie held up five fingers for her family. Then she put down one for Max. He still sat in a high chair, so he didn't really count. Then she put one up for Kate, and one for Ms. Moffly, and one for Mr. Bloom. That was seven. She counted once more. Yep. Seven. For sure.

So why were there eight places at the table? Her mom must have counted wrong. Unless...

Oh, no!

Unless someone had asked if they could bring their own date and Sophie's mom had said yes!

Then Sophie would have to get rid of the date. Right away. But how? She looked at the extra plate. She could always take it off. And the extra chair. She could hide it. If the date couldn't sit down, then there was no way the date could stay. . . .

But before she could do anything, Sophie heard a soft *ding-dong*.

The doorbell!

Her mom called, "Hey, Sophie, could you please—"

But Sophie was already in the front hall. She

pulled open the door. There was Kate in her best dress. Sophie hugged her. "Hi!"

"Hi, Sophie!" said Kate's mom. She was beside Kate, holding a tray. "My goodness! You look so fancy! Do you think I look okay?"

Sophie shrugged and nodded. "Yes." She looked fine, Sophie guessed, for dropping off Kate.

Then her own mom walked up and hugged Kate's mom. "Susan! Come on in! I'm so glad you could come!"

Ah! Sophie added that up. So Kate's mom was number eight. *Phew!* Plus she'd brought her special brownies. They had chocolate chips inside. And mint icing on top. *Yum!*

Kate's mom followed Sophie's mom into the kitchen just as the doorbell rang again.

"We got it!" Sophie hollered. *Oh, boy!* This was it.

Sophie made sure her jewels were perfect. Kate made sure her socks were up. Then they flung the door open together.

"Hi there!" said Mr. Bloom.

He still had on his bike helmet. And jeans, of course. But in his hand was a big bunch of yellow roses. *Mmm!* Sophie could smell them from the porch.

He's no Prince Charming, thought Sophie. But the flowers helped. A lot.

"Hi, Mr. Bloom," she said. "I'm Sophie, Hayley's sister. Remember me?"

He grinned and reached out to shake her hand. "Ms. Moffly's little snake charmer!" He winked. "How could I forget?"

Sophie blushed. She wished he *would* forget about the time she'd borrowed the snake from his classroom. She needed to change the subject. Fast.

"This is my best friend, Kate," she said. "She's also in Ms. Moffly's class."

Mr. Bloom gave Kate's hand a shake, too. "Pleased to meet you, Kate."

"Ms. Moffly likes to shake hands, too!" said Sophie. "We both *love* her. Don't we, Kate?"

"Oh, yeah!" Kate nodded hard. "She's the

best teacher we've ever had! She'd make a great wife, I bet!"

It was Sophie's turn to nod. "I agree! Are those flowers for her, by any chance?"

"These?" Mr. Bloom looked at his roses. "Oh, no, these just help me ride my bike."

Huh?

"How?" asked Sophie and Kate together.

"I use the *petals*." Mr. Bloom grinned.

Sophie smiled. *Ha!* She got it.

Kate laughed and laughed.

Just then, Sophie's mom walked out. "Mr. Bloom, hello! Girls, stand back and let the poor man in!" She took the roses he offered her. "Why, thank you. They're beautiful!"

Then she took his arm. "Come into the kitchen. There's someone you just *have* to meet!"

Sophie watched them go, then turned to Kate. "Okay, now where's Ms. Moffly?" she asked.

Kate held up her finger. "Hey, I think I hear a car!"

They peeked through the front window. *Yes!* A car was pulling up.

It stopped and the door opened.

"Who's that?" said Kate.

"I don't know." Sophie shrugged.

Wait. Maybe she did.

She gasped. "It's Ms. Moffly!"

Sophie and Kate looked at each other and clapped their hands over their mouths. Sophie could tell they were thinking the very same thing: *I can't believe that's our teacher!*

She had her hair up and everything! And shoes with high, pointy heels! The girls opened the door and ran out to meet her. Then they each grabbed a hand and dragged her in.

"Look who's here, everyone!" Sophie cried.

All the grown-ups came out of the kitchen.

"Oh, dear," Ms. Moffly said, looking around. "I'm overdressed. Aren't I?"

"Oh, no! You're not!" Sophie smoothed her own dress, then she glanced at her mom. "My mom looks as nice as she's ever going to get."

Kate nodded. "Yeah. Mine, too."

The moms looked at each other. "Thanks a lot!" They both laughed.

Sophie sighed. "I think you look beautiful, Ms. Moffly. Just like a bride! Don't you think so, Mr. Bloom?"

"Uh...yes." He nodded. "Very pretty."

A happy tingle bounced through Sophie. "And wait till you *smell* her!" she went on.

"Okay...well..." Sophie's dad clapped his hands together. "I'm hungry!" he declared. "And that lasagna smells delicious, as always. Don't you think we should eat, dear?"

He turned to Sophie's mom. She was busy giving Sophie a funny look. "Hmm?" she said. "Oh, yes. Let's go into the dining room, everyone."

Sophie and Kate let the grown-ups go first.

Sophie sniffed. "I think I smell something else!"

Kate looked confused. "What?" She leaned in.

Sophie hooked her arm through Kate's. "I think love is in the air!"

CHAPTER 10

Well, it wasn't the best date ever, Sophie decided. But it also wasn't the worst.

Yes, the birthday candles burned out in two minutes. "Now we know how long they last!" her dad joked. But the dark gave Sophie's bracelets a good chance to glow.

And Max stayed in his high chair almost the whole time. That was all thanks to Mr. Bloom, who had the idea to give him his phone.

"He's going to eat it," Sophie warned.

But to her surprise, he did not. Instead, Max

figured out how to play a game and got the all-time highest score.

If only Sophie had remembered to have some music during dinner. *Ugh!* But she didn't think of it till halfway through. Too bad.

To make up for it, she started to hum the wedding song: *"Hummm hummm hmm-hummmm..."* It was the most romantic song she knew. But that didn't last long. She stopped when her mom shot her one of those slightly scary, "Stop that right now, Sophie!" looks.

Still, Sophie could tell the teachers were having a great time. And she could almost hear their wedding toast: "To Sophie the Sweetheart!" they'd say. "Without her, our Number One Flower Girl, we wouldn't all be here today!"

Then Sophie would curtsy in her special dress—one with a long, poofy skirt. And she'd take Kate's and Hayley's hands and say, "Don't forget! They were there, too!"

The meal went so fast, Sophie could hardly

believe it when dinner was over and dessert was served.

"That was delicious," said Ms. Moffly.

"And I love these brownies!" said Mr. Bloom.

"Yes, aren't they good?" Sophie's mom grinned. "Susan makes the best brownies in the whole neighborhood."

If only this date could go on and on and on! Sophie thought.

Then she got an idea.

"Hey! Who wants to square dance?" Dinner and dancing. Now *that* was a date!

"Square dance?" her dad repeated. He shared a look with Sophie's mom.

"That's a fun idea," said Ms. Moffly.

Yes!

"But I'm afraid I have to go."

Aw!

Ms. Moffly looked down at her watch. "My boyfriend's company's also having a party tonight," she said. "And I said I'd try to stop by."

WHAT?!

Had Sophie heard right? She spun to look at Kate.

Yep. Kate was making the same *"No way!"* face. And Hayley was, too.

Suddenly, all the pictures in her mind of Ms. Moffly and Mr. Bloom's big wedding popped and fizzled away. Sophie was going to have some very, very disappointing news for her class on Monday.

And poor Mr. Bloom! His heart must be broken now, Sophie thought. She turned to him. Yes, he was about to cry.

Or . . . wait.

Was he about to *laugh*?

Was he telling Kate's mom a joke? And was she laughing back?

Oh, who cared. Sophie pulled off her earrings. *Looks like I got all dressed up for no reason at all.*

☆   ☆   ☆

No, things had not turned out as Sophie had planned. But in the end, they weren't *so* bad.

At least Ms. Moffly had a boyfriend. So maybe

there would be a wedding after all. And maybe the whole class would still be invited. And Ms. Moffly would still need some flower girls....

Sophie grinned as fancy dresses swirled back into her mind. But then she noticed her mom's smile. It was even bigger than hers. Why?

Sophie looked up from the sofa. Tiptoe was stretched out across her skirt. Her mom and dad had just finished a two-person job called Putting Max to Bed. Hayley was on the computer, pretty much ignoring all of them. She was probably chatting with Kim about dinner...and boys, too, of course.

"I just *knew* Mike and Susan would hit it off," Sophie's mom told her dad.

He crossed his arms and raised an eyebrow. "Don't tell me that was your plan?"

Her mom shrugged a "maybe" shrug. Then she winked a "you bet" wink.

Hang on! Sophie stared at her mother. Had she been matchmaking, too?! *No way!* Sophie thought at first. Mr. Bloom and Kate's *mom*? *Ew!*

But on second thought... *Hmm.* Kate and her mom did live all by themselves. And Mr. Bloom was kind of funny. And not bad at shaking hands.

And, hey! If they got married, that could mean *two* weddings in Sophie's future... and Kate's.

Yes!

Sophie guessed her only real problem now was the same one as always—her name. Was she still Sophie the Sweetheart? And did she still want to be? (And did that mean she'd have to be sweet to *Archie Dolan* one day?!)

"What are you thinking about, sweetheart?" her mom asked. She sat down by Sophie on the couch.

Her dad sat on her other side and hugged her shoulder tight.

"Oh, the usual," Sophie said. She smiled up at them both.

Whoever she was, she was a sweetheart to *them*, and that was very nice to know.